W9-AQB-984

EJ PENDZIWOL 2017
Pendziwol, Jean,
Me and you and the red canoe /

Montville Township Public Library
90 Horseneck Road
Montville, N.J. 07045-9626
973-402-0900
<u>Library Hours</u>
Monday   9 a.m. - 9 p.m.
Tuesday   9 a.m. - 9 p.m.
Wednesday   9 a.m. - 9 p.m.
Thursday   9 a.m. - 9 p.m.
Friday   9 a.m. - 6 p.m.
Saturday   9 a.m. - 5 p.m.
Sunday   12 p.m. - 5 p.m.
see website www.montvillelibrary.org

Text copyright © 2017 by Jean E. Pendziwol
Illustrations copyright © 2017 by Phil
Published in Canada and the USA in 2017 by Groundwood Books

All rights reserved. No part of this publication may be reproduced, stored
in a retrieval system or transmitted, in any form or by any means, without
the prior written consent of the publisher or a license from The Canadian
Copyright Licensing Agency (Access Copyright). For an Access Copyright
license, visit www.accesscopyright.ca or call toll free to 1-800-893-5777.

Groundwood Books / House of Anansi Press
groundwoodbooks.com

We acknowledge for their financial support of our publishing program the
Canada Council for the Arts, the Ontario Arts Council and the Government
of Canada.

  Canada Council   Conseil des Arts
for the Arts   du Canada

ONTARIO ARTS COUNCIL
CONSEIL DES ARTS DE L'ONTARIO
an Ontario government agency
un organisme du gouvernement de l'Ontario

With the participation of the Government of Canada
Avec la participation du gouvernement du Canada | Canadä

Library and Archives Canada Cataloguing in Publication
Pendziwol, Jean, author
Me and you and the red canoe / Jean E. Pendziwol ; illustrated by Phil.
Issued in print and electronic formats.
ISBN 978-1-55498-847-1 (hardcover). — ISBN 978-1-55498-848-8 (PDF)
I. Phil, illustrator II. Title.
PS8581 E55312 M4 2017   jC813'.54   C2016-908003-X
C2016-908004-8

The illustrations were done in acrylic on panel.
Design by Michael Solomon
Printed and bound in Malaysia

To the MacLuPen paddlers who shared
many wonderful canoe trips,
Erin, Krista, Colin, Phil, Zachary,
Stuart, Ryan and Anna,
and the gouvernail who led and
fed them, Frank, Nancy, James and
Karol. JEP

The family that canoes together stays
together.
To my backpack and canoe portage
crew — my wife Monica and my
children Gabriel, Allegra and Lukas —
traversing the many lakes of Ontario's
Algonquin Park. P

me and you
and the red canoe

Jean E. Pendziwol   *pictures by Phil*

 GROUNDWOOD BOOKS   HOUSE OF ANANSI PRESS   TORONTO   BERKELEY

I WOKE before the sun was up,
before the moon closed its eyes,
before the stars twinkled out,
when the whole world was just thinking
about the new day,
and everything was
purple and magical.

You were already awake,
listening to the chorus of frogs,
dressed, waiting.
You smiled,
winked
and held a finger to your lips.

We crawled from the tent
carefully,
quietly,
so we didn't wake the others.

I stretched and yawned.

You lit the fire,
smoke coiling up
all the way to the top of the pines
that stood guarding our campsite,
black pointy shadows
reaching to the sky.

We sat on a log by the shore,
sipping hot chocolate
from warm mugs,
listening to the laughter of a loon
calling out from the mist.

I carried our rods.

You carried the tackle and bait.

We pushed our red canoe out onto the lake.

I sat in the bow,
my paddle dipping
in and out,
in and out,
in and out.

You sat in the stern,
your paddle keeping time.
A trail of ripples traced our path through the water,
past the rocky cliff and around the point,
into the bay.

We paused,
silent,
drifting in our red canoe,
and watched a moose
on long gangly legs
pluck cattails from the shallows
for his breakfast.

I dropped my line
into the blue-green depths,
my lure
spinning,
twirling,
dancing.

You paddled.

We waited.

I jumped when a loud
thwack!
slapped nearby and
echoed
back and forth.

You pointed at the beaver,
sleek and brown,
swimming with a stick
to repair her home.

We heard a squirrel scolding,
chit,
chit,
chattering,
telling the waking forest
we were there.

I felt,
maybe,
a tug
and checked my line,
but it was only a weed
clinging to the hook.
I cleaned it off
and sent it back to the blue-green depths,
spinning,
twirling,
dancing.

You paddled.

We waited.

I watched the sun
poke through the trees,
sending golden ribbons
across the lake.

You pointed out a nest
high atop a leafless birch,
and not far away
the white head
and dark body
and piercing yellow eyes
of the eagle.

We wondered how
all those twigs and sticks
and other bits
survived the wind and rain.

I checked my line.
Again.

You paddled.

We waited.

And then...

I felt
tug,
tug,
TUG...

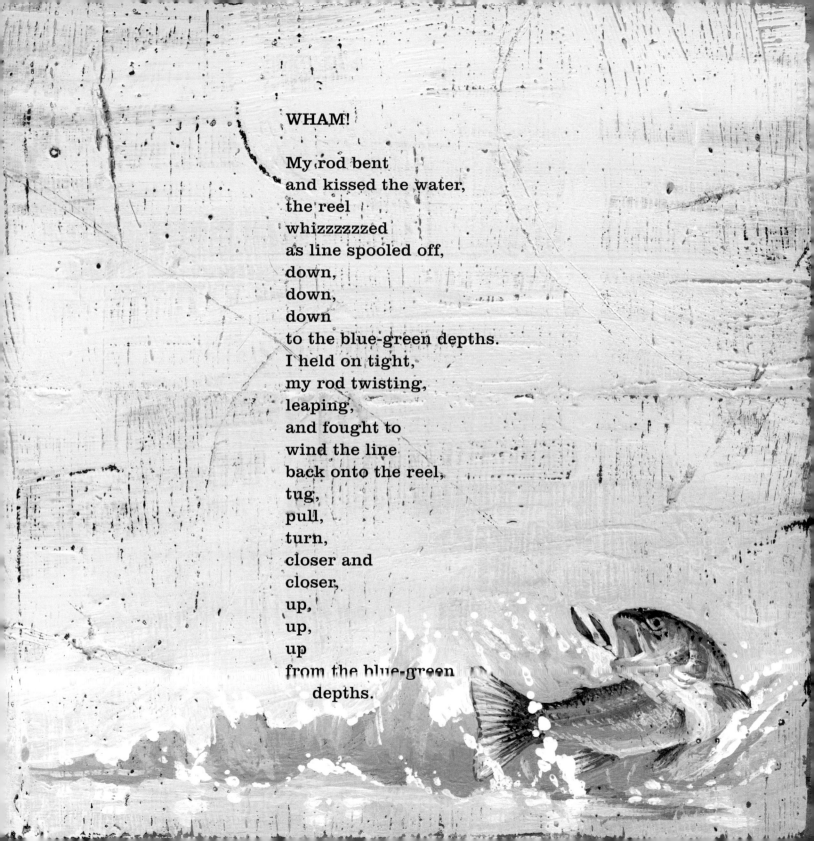

WHAM!

My rod bent
and kissed the water,
the reel
whizzzzzzed
as line spooled off,
down,
down,
down
to the blue-green depths.
I held on tight,
my rod twisting,
leaping,
and fought to
wind the line
back onto the reel,
tug,
pull,
turn,
closer and
closer,
up,
up,
up
from the blue-green
depths.

It was just
me and the fish
fighting,
while the moose browsed
and the beaver worked
and the squirrel scolded
and the eagle watched,
forgotten.

Then silver leapt from
water to sky,
soared from
sky to water
and landed with a splash
beside the red canoe.

You dipped the net into the lake.

We landed the trout.

I sat in the bow,
my paddle dipping
in and out,
in and out,
in and out.

You sat in the stern,
your paddle keeping time,
the sunlight sparkling in our wake.

We heard laughter,
the knock of ax against wood,
smelled coffee and bacon
and smoke from the fire,
saw the others
stretching and yawning
as we beached the red canoe
and jumped ashore.

I put another log on the fire
and stirred the coals
until they glowed
hot.

You cleaned the fish
and fried it up in butter,
golden and crispy.

We agreed
it was the
best breakfast
ever.